NIGHTS AT THE ALEXANDRA

# The Harper Short Novel Series

————————————

# WILLIAM TREVOR

## NIGHTS AT THE ALEXANDRA

ILLUSTRATIONS BY PAUL HOGARTH

PERENNIAL LIBRARY

Harper & Row, Publishers, *New York*
*Cambridge, Philadelphia, San Francisco*
*London, Mexico City, São Paulo, Singapore, Sydney*

*Nights at the Alexandra* originally appeared under the title "Frau Messinger" in *The New Yorker*.

A hardcover edition of this book was published in 1987 by Harper & Row, Publishers.

First PERENNIAL LIBRARY edition published 1988.

DESIGNED BY LYDIA LINK

Library of Congress Cataloging-in-Publication Data

Trevor, William, 1928–
  Nights at the Alexandra.

  (The Harper short novel series)
  "Perennial Library."
  I. Title.
  PR6070.R4N54   1988        823'.914        87-45349
ISBN 0-06-091513-7 (pbk.)

88 89 90 91 92 FG 10 9 8 7 6 5 4 3 2 1

# NIGHTS AT THE ALEXANDRA

# ONE

*I* AM A FIFTY-EIGHT-YEAR-OLD provincial. I have no children. I have never married.

'Harry, I have the happiest marriage in the world! Please, when you think of me, remember that.'

That is what I hear most often and with the greatest pleasure: Frau Messinger's voice as precisely recalled as memory allows, each quizzical intonation reflected in a glance or gesture. I must have replied something, Heaven knows what: it never mattered because she rarely listened. The war had upset the Messingers' lives, she being an Englishwoman and he German. It brought them to Ireland and to Cloverhill — a sanctuary they most certainly would not otherwise have known. She explained to me that she would not have found life comfortable in Hitler's Germany; and her own country could hardly be a haven for her husband. They had thought of Switzerland, but Herr Messinger believed that Switzerland would be invaded; and the United States did not tempt them. No one but I, at that time an unprepossessing youth of fifteen, ever used their German titles: in the town where I'd been born they were Mr and Mrs Messinger, yet it seemed to me — affectation, I daresay — that in this way we should honour the strangers that they were.

When first I heard of the Messingers I had just returned from the Reverend Wauchope's rectory, where I lodged in term-time in order to attend Lisscoe grammar school. My father told me about them. He said the man was twice the woman's age; he imagined they were Jews since they attended no church. A lot of Jews had slipped away from Germany, he ponderously added.

As a matter of principle, I refused to be interested in anything my father related, but a few days later I saw Frau Messinger stepping out of her husband's motor-car in Laffan Street and guessed at once who she was. The motor-car was powered by propane gas, a complicated apparatus being mounted where part of the luggage compartment had been removed: no one had petrol to spare during what in Ireland we called the 'Emergency', and energy so ingeniously contrived was rare. A group of loiterers had gathered round the motor-car. Frau Messinger paid them no attention.

'Will you carry something for me?' she said to me, and pointed at the wet battery of a wireless-set on the floor by the passenger seat. 'Might I ask you to carry it to the garage, and bring the other back?'

It is odd to think that those were the first words I heard her speak. Other boys had previously undertaken this chore: for some particular reason of her own she chose not to drive into Aldritt's garage and have the used battery replaced there by the one that had been recharged. Vaguely, she referred to that when she returned to the motor-car with her shopping, something about it being less of a nuisance like this. She opened the passenger door and showed me how to wedge the battery to prevent it from toppling over. 'I'd really be most awfully lost without the wireless,' she said, giving me a threepenny-piece.

She was an extremely thin, tall woman, her jet-black hair piled high, her eyes blue, her full lips meticulously painted: I had never seen anyone as beautiful, nor heard a voice that made me so deliciously shiver. *You looked for a blemish on her hands, on the skin of her neck or her face*, I wrote in a notebook I kept later in my life. *There wasn't one. I could have closed my eyes and listened to that husky timbre for ever.*

'There is something that hasn't come in to Kickham's,' she said. 'It's due on the bus this afternoon. Might I ask you to bring it out to Cloverhill for me?'

I remember that more distinctly than any other moment in my life. She was already in the car when she spoke, and her tone of voice was not one normally employed when making a request. With a gentle imperiousness, she commanded what she wished, and before she drove away she glanced at me once, a smile flittering across her thin features. The street-corner loiterers watched the slow progress of the car until it was out of sight, and then returned to lean again against the corner of Duggan's public house. I stood where I was, still aware of tremors dancing beneath my skin.

'What kind of a female is she?' my father enquired when he discovered – not from me – that I'd been addressed by Frau Messinger on the street. He was surprised when I told him that in my opinion she was an Englishwoman. He insisted I was mistaken, just as later he refused to accept that the Messingers were not Jews: in times like these, he said, no Englishwoman in her sane mind would marry a Hun, it stood to reason. 'Amn't I right?' he persuaded my mother, and she – not really listening – said he was of course.

We were a Protestant family of the servant class which had come up in the world, my father now the proprietor of the timberyard where he had once been employed. He was a bulky man, inclined to knock things over; he thought of himself as easygoing and wise. My mother's hands were swollen and red from washing clothes and floors and dishes;

her greying fair hair was forever slipping out of its hairpins. My two grandmothers, who lived with us, had not addressed one another since my parents' wedding-day. My two brothers, younger than I was, were chunkily-built twins, their identities often confused even within the family. My sister Annie — already working in the office of the timberyard — was jealous because I had been sent away to the grammar school at Lisscoe and she had not, and because my brothers would be sent away also. She resented the dullness of the employment she was so often told she was lucky to have. She wanted to work in a shop in Dublin.

Our house was the last building in Laffan Street except for the sheds and concrete stores of the timberyard next door. It was a pale brown house, of painted stucco, without railings to separate it from the pavement and without steps in front of its hall-door. The windows of its three storeys had net curtains as well as heavier curtains and blinds. The narrow, steep stairway that ascended from the hall to the attics was a central vein, supplying access to trim, short landings on the first and second floors. There was an upstairs sitting-room that was never used, the kitchen and the dining-room forming between them the household's heart. My brothers spread their schoolbooks out on the dining-room table, as Annie and I had once upon a time done also. The kitchen adjoined, with a hatch in the wall for convenience. My grandmothers sat in two armchairs by the dining-room window, watching the people going by on the street; in cold weather they sat on either side of the fire, not looking at one another. When we were small Annie and I used to share a bedroom, but now we had one each: patterned linoleum on the floor, an iron bedstead, wash-stand and cupboard, just like our parents' bedroom and our brothers'.

These rooms, the steep stairway and the landings, the square backyard you could see from the bedroom windows, its red outhouse doors and the sloping roof of its turf shed: all that constituted my familiar childhood world, and the town that lay beyond this territory of home reflected it in many ways, though at the time I did not notice this. It was a scrappy, unimportant little town, a handful of shops and public houses in narrow streets, its central square spoilt by two derelict houses and a statue to a local martyr. Bridge Quay and Bridge Lane ran off Laffan Street; Nagle Street was where Reilly's Café and the two better grocers' shops were, separated by Kickham's drapery. The Wolfe Tone Dance-hall resembled a repository for agricultural implements — a relentless cement façade halfway up Wolfe Tone Hill, with a metal grille drawn across by day, the week's band announced on a bill stuck to a nearby telegraph pole. On the outskirts of the town was the Church of Our Lady, and at the end of St Alnoth Street the slender spindle of the Protestant Church of St Alnoth was dark against the sky.

I walked through the town on the first of my journeys to Cloverhill, clutching a soft, brown-paper parcel from Kickham's. I wondered what it contained and tried to feel beneath the string and the overlap of paper, but was not successful. I felt excited, quickening my stride as I passed the abandoned gasworks and the hospital that was being built, branching to the right at the signpost where the road divided. *Ballinadee* the signpost said, 2½ *miles*. The road became narrow then, and there were no cottages all the way to the white gates of Cloverhill, which were set in a crescent sweep bounded by a stone wall. An avenue meandered through fields where sheep grazed except where the land had been ploughed. From the moment I passed through the gates I could see the house in the distance, in grey, stern stone against treeless landscape.

Astride a farm horse, a man rode towards me. 'You have come with my wife's ordering,' he said. 'You are good to her.' He was a small, square man, too muscular to be described as fat, with short sandy hair and a drooping eyelid. Agreeably, he asked me my name and where I lived. When I told him my father was the proprietor of the timberyard he replied that that was interesting. He himself, he informed me before he passed on, cultivated sugar-beet mainly.

The fields on either side of the avenue became uncared-for lawns, with flower-beds in them. There was a gravel sweep, steps led to a white hall-door. I pulled the bell-chain and heard, a moment later, the tap of the maid's heels on the flagged floor of the hall. At Cloverhill, I discovered later, the Messingers lived with this single servant, a girl of seventeen or eighteen with attractively protruding teeth, called Daphie. Two farm-workers, one of them her father, came by day. In the Messingers' marriage no children had been born.

I was led into the drawing-room, where Frau Messinger was sitting on a green-striped sofa, made comfortable with green-striped cushions bunched into the corner behind her. She was smoking a cigarette. As on all future occasions when I visited her in this room, she wore red, this time a scarlet dress of a soft woollen material, with a black silk scarf knotted loosely at her throat. In other ways, also, it was always just the same: I would enter the elegantly furnished drawing-room and be subjected to wide-eyed, frank appraisal, an examination that was accompanied by a smile. She never said much at first. When the tea was brought she poured it and at once lit a fresh cigarette, then leaned back against her cushions, her eyes not leaving my face, her smile still lingering. Sometimes, for an instant before she settled herself, the black lace hem of her petticoat showed. Then she would tidy her skirt about her knees and the lacy hem would not again be seen.

'This is kindness itself,' she said that first time. 'Boys are not often kind.'

I deprecated her compliment, but was ignored. A silence fell. She guessed my age, and said that she herself was twenty-seven, her husband sixty-two. I did not, at the time, find anything odd in that; I did not think of Frau Messinger as a girl, which is how I remember her now, nor of her husband as an old man, which later he appeared to me to be. All that seemed peculiar to me then was that we just drank tea: there was nothing to eat, not even a sandwich or a biscuit.

'Both of us were born beneath the sign of Sagittarius,' she said. Not that she entirely believed in the astrology notes she read in magazines, yet she could not quite resist them. 'Do *you* like reading just for fun?' she asked and then, not waiting for an answer, described the various German and French magazines that had delighted her when she'd lived in Germany. What she'd enjoyed most of all was drinking afternoon chocolate in a café and leafing through the pages of whatever journals were there. She described a café in a square in Münster where the daily newspapers were attached to mahogany rods that made them easier to read, and where there were magazines on all the tables. Guessing that I had never been in a theatre, she described the orchestra and the applause, the painted scenery, the make-up and the actors. She described a cathedral in Germany, saying she and Herr Messinger had been married in it. 'Harry, do you think you could save me a horrid journey and bring out the wet battery from Aldritt's on Tuesday?'

This was the indication that my present visit had come to

an end. There was the lavish smile, and the assumption that naturally I would agree to carry out the wireless battery. Without hesitation, I said I would.

'I hear you were at Cloverhill,' my father remarked that evening, when all of us were gathered around the dining-table from which we ate our meals. The family atmosphere was as it always was: my grandmothers silent in their dislike of one another, my brothers sniggering, my mother tired, Annie resentful, my father ebullient after an hour or so in the back bar of Viney's hotel.

'Cloverhill?' Annie said, her lips pouting in a spasm of jealousy. 'Were you out at Cloverhill?'

'I had a message from Kickham's.'

'So you'd say they were Jews?' my father said.

I shook my head. Since the Messingers had been married in a cathedral it seemed unlikely that they could be Jewish. He came from a village near a town called Münster, I said; she was definitely English.

'Well, I'd say they were Jews.' My father cut a slice of shop bread with the bread-saw, scattering crumbs from the crust over the table-cloth. 'The Jew-man goes to the synagogue. There's no synagogue in this town.'

My father lent his observations weight through his slow delivery of them, his tone suggesting revelations of import yet to come. But invariably this promise remained unfulfilled.

'I'm surprised you were running messages for them,' my sister said.

I did not reply. I would tell my companions at the Reverend Wauchope's rectory – Mandeville, Houriskey and Mahoney-Byron – about the Messingers: it was clearly no use attempting to convey anything about them to any member of my family. One of my brothers upset a cup of tea, and with a vigour that belied the weariness in her features my mother delivered a slap to the side of his face. The less squat of my grandmothers exclaimed her approval; the other muttered in distaste. The subject of the Messingers did not survive this interruption; my father talked about the war.

On Tuesday I collected the charged battery at Aldritt's garage and carried it out to Cloverhill. It was made of glass, and fitted into a wire cage with a handle: it wasn't difficult to carry, nor was it heavy. Frau Messinger gave me a list that afternoon, and the packets and the single parcel I conveyed to Cloverhill two days later were hardly a burden either. Then it was time to collect from Aldritt's the battery I had myself left there a week before. I even learnt how to connect the wires of the wireless-set to it.

'Harry, I should like to tell you a little about my mother and myself,' Frau Messinger said on the last afternoon of my holidays, a warm afternoon in September when the French windows of her drawing-room were wide open. A bumblebee buzzed intermittently, alighting on one surface after another, silent for a moment before beginning its next flight. The last bumblebee of summer, she said, and added without any change of voice, as though the same subject continued:

'My mother was a poor relation, Harry. From my earliest childhood that was an expression that accompanied us every-where we went. Often, in Sussex, my mother would wave one of her tiny hands at the landscape and announce that it was the family's. I also distinctly recall her doing so on the sea-front at Bognor Regis, implying with her delicate little wave all the houses of the promenade, and the seashore as well.'

She handed me the stub of her cigarette and asked me to take it to the garden and throw it away, out of sight somewhere, poked down into a flower-bed, she suggested. It was the first time she made this request of me, but she was often to make it in the future: the smell of stale cigarettes was unpleasant in a room, she explained, answering the bewilderment on my face.

'You naturally wonder about my father,' she said when I returned. 'Who he was and why he was never with us. Well, I'll tell you, Harry: I never knew my father. I never so much as laid an eye on him or heard his voice or even saw a photograph. My father was a dark horse. My mother wore a wedding ring, but I am honestly not sure that she did so with any title. I rather believe my father was something dreadful, like a pantryman.'

I did not know what a pantryman was, nor do I to this day. But I could tell from the lowered voice accompanying the revelation that in Frau Messinger's view a pantryman was a long way down the scale from a butler, or even a footman. Her mother had become enamoured of a lesser servant.

'My mother, no matter what else she was, Harry, was a very foolish little person. If she had not been foolish about some tedious investment she would not have become a poor relation. She was taken in by a solicitor in Sevenoaks who claimed he could make a fortune for her. She was lucky to have ended up with anything at all left. But not enough for my education.'

Her cigarette-lighter was round, like a polished gold coin. Sometimes she played with it while she talked. Sometimes she took a cigarette from her yellow Gold Flake packet, then changed her mind and returned it, tidily folding the silver paper as it had been folded before.

'My mother stayed in people's houses: that's how we lived. We went from house to house, in a circle all over Sussex, and when we arrived at a certain point we began all over again. Governesses taught me, Harry. I was passed from schoolroom to schoolroom in the houses where we stayed, from Miss Kindle to Miss D'Arcy, to Miss Moate, to Miss Hindhassett, on to Miss Binding and Miss Gubbins. To tell the truth, Harry, I'm hardly educated at all. I mean, a smattering. I have nothing more.'

I formed a picture of the existence she described, of arriving with her mother and their luggage in this house or that, endlessly beholden. I saw her as the child she'd been, much taller than her mother, just as she was taller than her husband: a thin, lanky child was what she'd said, not very happy. I knew nothing of the kind of houses she spoke of, and imagined palaces in soft English countryside, with gardeners and parlour maids. She and her mother travelled by train, and someone met them at the railway station. Often it wasn't actually a railway station but a special stopping place in the middle of nowhere, a 'halt', she called it, used only by the people of the nearby estate.

Even now, so very long afterwards, I can clearly see the clothes she described to me: her favourite dress when she was twelve, in forget-me-not blue with tiny white dots that were flowers when you looked closer, and plain white buttons; her favourite dress when she was fifteen, of crimson velvet, the first of her red dresses; the lace stole she was given once; green shoes she'd had. Furniture in the houses she'd visited remained vivid in her recollection, and has passed into mine: a Queen Anne dressing-glass of inlaid rosewood, so delicately finished that she had always had difficulty in drawing her eyes away from it; a gold-faced clock on a mantelpiece in a hall; pale Chippendale chairs around an oval table. On the day after her eighteenth birthday a young man had proposed marriage to her, and she wept because she loved him but even so rejected him. They had walked together through a meadow where poppies bloomed, then by a river and an apple orchard. That year she had learnt Italian. That year she had tried particularly to be good at tennis, which she had always wanted to be. At nineteen she had become religious, and had wondered about the Virgin Mary and the mystery of the Annunciation.

'You will wonder why we were in Germany, Harry. Well, it's the same kind of thing as staying in other people's houses. Mrs Marsh-Hall needed a companion to travel with, her sister having died the previous year. So she took my mother with her as well as a maid, and of course I was permitted to go along. Otherwise I would never have met my husband.'

When she spoke of that time Frau Messinger uttered a few words in German before returning to English to tell me about her husband's many sisters and his cousin who was unable to speak because of a stroke, his niece who'd been a singer and lived with the family in their *Schloss*. Herr Messinger had been left a widower seven or eight years ago; he had three sons in Hitler's army.

'None of it is nice for him, Harry. "You must buy land with the house in Ireland," I said. "You must be occupied." For my husband, idleness is a penance.'

She offered me a cigarette, the first time she had done so. She held out the packet casually, appearing not to consider it unusual that a boy of fifteen should smoke. I accepted it because at the grammar school I often smoked behind the lavatories.

'My mother died, Harry, or else you would have met her. She would have come here with us, I think.'

Her tone was not melancholy. She seemed happy to have only Herr Messinger. People had come to call when she had first arrived at Cloverhill, women mainly, bearing visiting cards to represent their husbands, since husbands tended to be occupied at that time of day.

'Of course I returned the calls, Harry. Well, really, it would be rude not to.'

But social life ended there. There were invitations to bridge and whist parties, but neither Frau Messinger nor her husband had any interest in card-playing.

'Yet of course we were right, Harry, to come to Ireland. We are proved right every day. Adolf Hitler apologised, you know, when a bomb fell out of one of his aeroplanes on to a creamery somewhere — in Co. Tipperary, was it?'

She didn't care for Adolf Hitler, nor did Herr Messinger, even though his sons were fighting for the Nazis. She had fallen in love with Germany and almost overnight Germany had become a tragedy.

'Old women sat in the cafés of Münster, Harry, their faces crinkled in despair at what they read in the newspapers and the magazines. And then the horrible Brownshirts would go by, goosestepping with their legs. You couldn't help loving the manners of the Germans, but what good were manners then?'

I held my cigarette as nonchalantly as I could, dangling it as she was dangling hers.

'It's such a disappointment, Harry, that people can be so silly. Don't you think it is?'

She went on talking, not waiting for my response. Herr Messinger could hardly bear even to think about the sadness that had befallen Germany. 'And poor England, too, Harry — those horrid bombs coming out of the darkness!'

The houses she had visited in Sussex were maybe in ruins by now. People lived on a rasher of bacon a month, and eggs made from powder. In England clothing wasn't warm enough. In Germany the elderly died.

'We're creatures of absurdity, you realise, my husband and myself. Creatures of ridicule, Harry, sitting out two countries' conflict.'

It hadn't been easy for her husband to come away, to leave his family behind, his sisters and his sons. When he read the news in the papers he wondered if they still survived.

'They are not permitted to communicate, Harry. We must wait to know until all this is over.'

She would have been arrested and sent to an internment camp in Germany, as Herr Messinger would have been in England. Every indignity that could be devised would have been visited on them. And the one remaining free would have been reviled for marrying the other.

'I am ashamed of my country when I think of that, Harry. As my husband is of his. That the innocent should be ill-treated, even allowed to die, in the glorious name of war: what kind of world have we made for ourselves?'

He had tried to persuade his sisters, and all the household of the *Schloss*, to accompany them to Ireland; his sons would not have been allowed to. But it was easier for his sisters to continue with the familiar than to embark upon the strangeness of a country they had scarcely heard of. And they were getting on in years, and less pessimistic about the future than their brother.

'So we came alone to our sanctuary, and live with the guilt of it, Harry. There is always guilt in running away.'

Listening to her voice, I found myself wondering what happened in the drawing-room after my afternoon visits. Did she lie for a little longer on the sofa and then rise from it to prepare a meal for her husband? It was hard to imagine her with her sleeves rolled up and an apron tied over her dress. She did not appear to belong in a kitchen, with meat and vegetables and bread-soda. Yet Daphie did not strike me as someone capable of preparing meals: Daphie belonged more with brushes and dusters and tins of Brasso. A long time later I discovered that Herr Messinger did all the cooking at Cloverhill.

'Always be gentle with my husband, Harry. Not just his country, but a way of life, has been destroyed by criminals. That is not pleasant for any man to bear, you know.'

She had never before spoken of Herr Messinger in this manner, and certainly I had not thought of him as someone with whom it was necessary to be gentle. Yet now, so long afterwards, I understand, for the pictures that filled his mind — his sons engaged in futile battles, the *Schloss* a barracks, the old women weeping in the cafés — must daily have felt like a canker consuming him.

'When I was young, Harry, far younger than you are now, I used to wonder what life was going to be like.' She smiled in her sudden way, her evenly-arranged teeth whitely glistening. She had imagined an existence in the English countryside, watching her mother growing old, collecting bone china. 'I always loved pretty things, Harry. Thimbles and tiny mantelpiece ornaments. Such little objects were always in the houses we stayed at, but of course they were never mine. My husband has made up for that.'

She showed me a cabinet full of *objêts d'art* that I had hardly noticed before, in the corner of the drawing-room. Some of the china was German, some English. 'Cheek by jowl, Harry, making the silly war seem sillier.'

In a small garden she would have grown anemones, which were her favourite flower. 'I did not see how I could marry, yet later I did of course.' She smiled but did not explain that further: why it was she had chosen Herr Messinger, having rejected the young Englishman whom I had so very clearly seen walking with her in the poppied meadow on the day after her eighteenth birthday, when there were tears on her cheeks because she was in love. Herr Messinger, with his lined, square face and his drooping eyelid, was different in every way from the dark-haired figure in a white cotton suit and panama hat I had imagined. 'It was impossible that my husband and I should not marry,' was all she said.

I left her reluctantly on the last day of my holidays, wondering who would fetch the glass batteries for her until I returned, hoping no one would. Her eyes smiled her own particular farewell at me as she lay languid on the sofa, a cigarette she had not yet lit between her fingers. The bumblebee was still in the room, darting between the two brass lamps that hung from the ceiling, settling on one glass globe and then the other, before again becoming restless.

As I walked through dwindling sunshine, down the avenue and out on to the empty road, strange fantasies possessed me. I saw with vividness the Messingers' marriage in the German cathedral, candles alight on the altar, guests mysterious in a twilight gloom. I heard the singing of a choir, and then the bridal couple were in their honeymoon bedroom, she still in her wedding-dress, he pouring champagne into glasses. They ate slices of their wedding cake and laughed in their happiness, defying the war that already threatened to deprive them of it.

# TWO

$A$T THE REVEREND Wauchope's rectory, in the bedroom I shared with Mandeville and Houriskey and Mahoney-Byron, I journeyed again to Cloverhill, as I do in my memories to this day. At the grammar school my inability to learn what I was required to learn was soothed by possessive daydreams, my failure to make sense of mathematical abstractions lightened. Although later I wished I had not, I described to my companions at the rectory Frau Messinger's flawless skin and the way she had of smiling when she looked at you, and her jet-black hair. I mentioned her perfectly painted lips. 'Holy Jesus!' Mandeville whispered, his voice reverent with envy; Houriskey wanted to know if I ever got a look up her skirts. At Lisscoe grammar school there was a lot of talk like that; all humour was soiled, double meanings were teased out of innocence. When I described the clothes Frau Messinger wore I could see from Mahoney-Byron's expression that, one by one, he lifted the garments from her body.

'You haven't a snap of her?' Mandeville asked quietly.

'There are only the wedding photographs in her bedroom.'

'Were you in her bedroom?'

'She showed me one time.'

'Jesus Christ, man!' Houriskey and Mahoney-Byron shouted, perfectly in unison, but Mandeville's reaction was more intense and private. Mandeville was an emaciated boy with spectacles, the ravages of a departed acne still evident about his nose and chin. He had wavy fair hair that he brushed back from his forehead, with a central parting. Mandeville was besotted by the younger of the two English princesses, an infatuation that had developed in him the ambition to find employment of some kind in Buckingham Palace. Houriskey and Mahoney-Byron were bigger, heavier boys, the sons of farmers.

'What'd she show you in the bedroom?' Houriskey asked.

'Nothing; only what it was like. She showed me every room in the house one time.'

'Why'd she do that?'

'Because she's bored, I suppose.'

'God, you bugger!'

It had not occurred to me until that moment that she was bored. 'Harry, would you like to see the house?' she had said, then led the way from room to room, pausing longest in the bedroom she shared with her husband. 'You can lie in bed, Harry, and listen to the birds.' It was a room in which, apart from a trouser-press and the pillow on which he rested his head, there was little trace of Herr Messinger. Her hairbrushes and her scent bottles were arranged among the silver-framed wedding photographs on the dressing-table; her dresses hung in a wardrobe which she opened; a row of her shoes stretched between the two windows, their toes neatly in line; her nightdress, silkily pale-green, lay on the candlewick eider-down; perfume scented the air.

'If she took you into her bedroom she was on for it,' Houriskey said. He laughed coarsely, at the same time as Mahoney-Byron. Mandeville smiled. Houriskey acquired jokes from an odd-job man on his father's farm and conveyed a stock of them to the school with each new term. They had to do with honeymoon couples, mislaid clothing, and intimacies concerning the odd-job man's wife. Raucous laughter emanated from Mahoney-Byron as each anecdote reached its conclusion, but Mandeville always only smiled.

'What's your man Messinger like?' Mahoney-Byron asked. 'Is he a spy?'

I described Herr Messinger. I said I doubted that he was a spy. Mahoney-Byron, who kept photographs of Hitler and Himmler between the pages of his Hall's Geometry, looked disappointed. 'Mr Churchill's stupidity', Mahoney-Byron liked to drawl in the mocking accents of Lord Haw-Haw, 'has led his island people to the brink of final destruction. There will not be a city street intact unless this addled old man ceases to feed falsehoods to a weary population.'

The rectory was situated beside the grammar school itself — two unadorned brick buildings in the middle of Lisscoe, which was a town more than twice the size of the one I knew so well but offering a similar provincial ambience. The lower panes of all the ground-floor windows of the school were painted white; in the rectory a smell of damp hung about the bare-board passages and the dining-room. On moist days this dampness penetrated to our bedroom, which was mostly occupied by our four beds and the pitchpine cupboard we kept our clothes in. 'We will pray to God,' the elderly Reverend Wauchope had said the first time he led us into this room — an insistence we were to become familiar with, the words demanding that, irrespective of whatever activity was taking place, those involved in it should fall at once to their knees. In her grimy basement kitchen the clergyman's wife vented a sour disposition on the food she cooked, assisted by a maid called Lottie Belle, whose inordinate stoutness contrasted dramatically with the spare frame of Mr Conron, the assistant master at the grammar school, who lodged at the rectory also. Mr Conron's wasted features were twisted in what appeared to be torment; his eyes were shifty.

While I talked about the Messingers in these surroundings and among these people, I sometimes felt I was relating a dream. The open French windows, the bumblebee and the scent of flowers, Herr Messinger astride his farm horse: all of it seemed so remote as to be outside the realms of existence. And why had they taken to me, awkward youth that I was? 'It's good you come, Harry,' Herr Messinger had said. 'A visitor is nice for her.' Did she miss me, I wondered, as I missed her? Did she remember me when she connected the wires to the battery?

'Did you never think of winking at the woman?' Houriskey suggested. 'You could be sitting there and give a wink that could be an accident.'

'I don't think she'd like being winked at.'

'God, you bugger!'

The four of us walked slowly around a field where cattle grazed, behind the red-brick rectory. When he'd said Grace in the dining-room that evening the Reverend Wauchope had kept us on our feet to announce the number of RAF planes that had returned from a bombing mission. He always did this when the news was good, permitting us to eat immediately when it was not. 'We will pray to God,' he had commanded, and while the grease congealed on the surface of his wife's mutton soup we sank to our knees, our arms clasped around the backs of our chairs in the manner ordained for dining-

room gratitude to the Almighty. Mahoney-Byron's plea for similar Luftwaffe success was kept low.

'Sure, why wouldn't he be a spy?' he persisted in the field, reminding me of my father's refusal to accept that the Messingers were not Jews. It was unlikely that a spy would be married to an Englishwoman, I said, but Mahoney-Byron told me to look for morse-code equipment in a barn, maybe hidden under a load of hay. 'There's a man in Dublin', he went on, 'with his house built in the shape of a swastika so's a Messerschmidt pilot would know where he was. Have a look in case your man has trees planted in the shape of a swastika. Or fences. Have a gander at the fences.'

We began our second circuit of the field. I could not see how spying might be engaged in from Cloverhill House but I did not say so; nor did I reveal that Herr Messinger had three sons in the Nazi army — for which the war at that time appeared to be going well. Norway and Denmark had capitulated. Holland, Belgium and France had fallen. The Messerschmidts Mahoney-Byron spoke of were clearly inflicting greater damage than radio commentators other than the notorious Lord Haw-Haw admitted: listeners at a distance made allowances for the fear that kept the truth obscure.

'I had a dream last night,' Mandeville murmured, removing his wire-rimmed spectacles and wiping them on the cuff of his jacket. His expression indicated that Cloverhill House and the Messingers were deemed exhausted as a conversational topic, at least for the time being. He coughed softly, which was a way of his. 'I was in a room with the King when she came in with a book in her hand. "What's that you're reading?" he says, only she's shy because of myself. But afterwards she comes up to me and says it's a poetry book. There's nothing she likes better than poetry.'

'Write her a letter,' Houriskey urged. 'She'd like to hear you were dreaming about her.'

'The day will come when I'll be telling her about this place, how I was thinking about her every hour that went by.'

'She'd be interested all right.'

As well as Mandeville's belief that he would find employment in Buckingham Palace, other vocational ambitions were aired from time to time. Houriskey's desire was to emigrate to the northern Canadian fishing grounds, a region for which he had developed an affection that puzzled us. Mahoney-Byron wished to pursue a talent he had for throwing his voice, investing inanimate objects, or creatures not normally so gifted, with speech. He believed he would find employment with Duffy's circus, and had contrived an act in which a number of giraffes engaged one another in conversation. As for myself, all I wanted was not to have to work in the timberyard. I would have readily agreed to become a schoolmaster like Mr Conron, or a post-office clerk or a meal-office clerk. But the timberyard and my father's ubiquitous presence in it, the endless whine of the saws, mud pitched up from the wheels of lorries, the rattle of rain on corrugated iron, the bitter odour of resin: that prospect appalled me, and I knew that what would accompany it within myself was the sullenness that had developed in my sister. 'Forty-one years I've been at it,' my father used to say, appropriately altering the reference as another year passed. He had worked in the yard as a child of ten; his own father had run around the town barefoot, the only Protestant child for twenty-nine miles so ill-clad. I dreaded the day when the hall-door would close behind both of us, when we would walk the few yards together to the timberyard, my sister Annie arriving later because the accounts shed didn't open until nine. Larchwood, beech, ash, oak dressed or left in its sawn condition, mahogany in short supply because of the Emergency: this would replace the dank corridors of the rectory and the white-painted classroom windows. At one o'clock I would return over the same few yards with my father and my sister, and my father would hold forth while we ate boiled bacon or chops. My grandmothers would ask him to repeat what all of us had already heard only too well; my brothers would snigger. There'd be semolina with a spoonful of blackberry jam, stewed rhubarb in season; there'd be Jacob's Cream Crackers with butter and Galtee cheese if my father was still hungry. That Jacob's invented the cream cracker was one of my father's greatly favoured mealtime statements.

'I have my little dotey with me here.' Mandeville produced from the back pocket of his trousers a grubby newspaper photograph of the princess. 'Is there a lovelier creature alive?'

We agreed that there wasn't and continued our walk in silence, each of us lost in fantasy. I might become a servant at Cloverhill House; I might keep the flower-beds tidy and the grass cut on the lawns; I might work in the fields with Herr Messinger. I wouldn't mind sitting in the kitchen with the young maid, taking my meals with her, and doing whatever they wanted me to do, growing anemones or lighting the fires every morning.

It snowed, surprisingly, in the autumn of that year. We stood around a coke stove in the hall of the rectory, endeavouring to keep warm, while in his homilies the Reverend Wauchope reminded us that thousands of British soldiers were sheltering under canvas, in temperatures far lower than those we were experiencing. The snow covered the huge hollow in front of the school where the town's dust carts dumped their cinders, the intention being that one day the level would reach that of the surrounding ground and allow for the laying out of a hockey pitch. Unfortunately the dust lorries occasionally committed the error of depositing a load of garbage, which was an attraction for rats and seagulls. At least the snow held in check the foetid odour of decay that normally drifted into the classrooms.

I imagined Frau Messinger suffering from the cold also, a rug drawn over her knees on the sofa in the drawing-room, the fingers that grasped her magazine so numb that she had to rub the life back into them. 'Daphie is good at fires,' she had said, but I guessed that in the big draughty rooms it would be chilly, no matter how vigorously the fires blazed. I imagined her husband in the frost-whitened landscape, felling trees and sawing them into logs. He and one of his men would go about the task in silence, skilfully working the cross-saw. Daphie would appear with a can of tea.

'Whatever's this stupid nonsense?' the Reverend Wauchope tetchily demanded one evening, sending for me specially. 'You're making yourself important, are you, with reports of German spies? That amounts to falsehood, you know.'

A rumour had got going in the grammar school, I endeavoured to explain. It was without foundation; it was simply that a German had come to live near the town I came from.

'Rumours are grapeshot for the enemy. We will pray to God.' I didn't listen to his voice, but imagined instead how astonished the Messingers would be if they could see us. She would laugh her tinkling laugh, her head thrown slightly back. He would shrug his shoulders in his expressive way.

'Stand up, man, stand up.' Renewed crossness interrupted my reflections, for I had remained on my knees longer than I should have. 'Your stupidity is a mockery of the human race. Go from my sight, boy.'

Castigated on one score by the Reverend Wauchope, I was approached on another by the assistant master. He sought me out when I was alone in a classroom, spoke first of the cold weather, made enquiries about my family, then said:

'There's talk of a certain nature that goes on between yourself and your friends.'

'What kind of talk's that, Mr Conron?'

'You know what I'm referring to. Involving women.'

I shook my head, instantly denying this.

'Mr Wauchope would not discuss things of that nature with you on account of he's a clergyman. So it falls to myself.'

'I understand, sir.'

'Mandeville carries a photograph of a woman around with him. There's a certain type of story Houriskey tells. There's stories you've made up yourself apparently.'

'Which stories are those, Mr Conron?'

He turned his tormented eyes away from me. In one of his trouser pockets he snapped a piece of chalk in half. His fingers emerged with one portion lightly held. He looked at it. Still doing so, he said:

'You have a pretence that you go to a house where there's a woman.'

'A pretence, Mr Conron?'

'Something you'd make up in your mind, the same as Mandeville with the photograph in his pocket. When you'd talk about a matter like that it would acquire a reality for you.'

I might have explained that, in fact, the opposite had occurred, but I did not do so. The assistant master said something I didn't hear and then referred to carnal temptation, enquiring as to my familiarity with it. 'Bad thoughts are at the root of carnal temptation. Things you'd pretend about.'

'I understand, sir.'

'It's best to avoid talk that would lead the way to it.'

'I'll take your advice, sir.'

Mr Conron regarded a stain on the boarded floor. In a voice so low that, again, I could hardly hear it he said:

'Did you ever pretend anything about Mrs Wauchope?'

I imagined, when I repeated this, Houriskey's and Mahoney-Byron's raucous laughter, and the intensity developing in Mandeville's expression. I shook my head. I had never pretended anything about Mrs Wauchope, I said; nor, since I was asked this too, about the maid, Lottie Belle.

The eyes closed, in relief or otherwise I had no way of knowing. 'Avoid anything like that,' Mr Conron advised, and I felt ashamed that I had ever spoken of Frau Messinger in the rectory or the school.

'Well, I'll tell you a queer thing,' my father said when I returned home at the end of that term. 'You'll never guess what I'm going to tell you.'

Ponderous head-wagging took place. I said I couldn't guess.

'There's talk of a picture house for the town. Did you ever hear the beat of that?'

I said I never had. There was money in a picture house, my father went on. Maguire the auctioneer had been going to build one nine years ago only he dropped dead. In the length and breadth of Ireland there wasn't a town of the same population that didn't possess a picture house. Didn't it take a cute old Hun to put his finger on the shame of it?

'D'you mean *he*'s going to build it?'

'Sure, we're a disgrace to the world,' my father said.

On Christmas Eve the town was crowded with people who had come in from the country, people you did not usually see on the streets. An old man in rags was playing an accordion, tinker women begged. Public houses were noisy, and as I walked down Laffan Street on my way to the Ballinadee road there was an air all around me of expectation and excitement. Soft misty rain had begun to fall; my clothes were wringing wet by the time I reached Cloverhill House.

'Stand by the fire,' Frau Messinger urged in the drawing-room. 'Oh, Harry, you are foolish! You could catch your death!'

Her husband, wearing riding breeches and gaiters, was crouched on the floor, poring over a mass of papers he had spread out on the fleur-de-lis pattern of the carpet. He was smoking a thin, black cigar and when he greeted me he confirmed what my father had said: he intended to build a cinema. The papers were the plans for its construction. It was a marriage gift for his wife, he said. She had asked for it specially.

'But, Harry, that site they offer me is not good. Too near the slum part of the town.'

Frau Messinger said hardly anything; she never did in her husband's presence. Instead she smiled with pleasure, delight-ing in his enthusiasm over the drawings on the carpet. His legs were tucked under him, a stubby finger indicated features of the proposed architecture. In the auditorium the seats would be tiered and there would be a balcony; most important of all, apparently, there would be Western Electric sound.

'On the curtains the pattern will be of butterflies, Harry.'

I did not know much about cinemas. Twice during my years at Lisscoe grammar school the Reverend Wauchope had granted permission for his boarders to attend Hussey's Picture House under the supervision of Mr Conron. We had sat enthralled, watching W. C. Fields and Edna May Oliver, and Charles Laughton in *Mutiny on the Bounty*. There'd been no balcony and no curtains such as Herr Messinger described; in the fourpenny seats gangs of ragged urchins had ceaselessly talked and whistled.

'This is where we've chosen instead, Harry.'

The cinema was to be where the two derelict houses stood in the square. It would transform the square, Herr Messinger promised, with baskets of plants hanging at intervals along the façade. *The Alexandra* announced towering letters on a sketch.

'Well, Harry, what do you think?'

'It's grand.'

'The idea is it should be grand. The box-office like so, stairs whichever side you prefer to mount to the balcony. Two usherettes.'

'Usherettes?'

'We have planned the dress: blue with gold on it, epaulettes to the shoulder.'

He showed me a sketch of a girl in such a uniform, then showed me other details: the mechanism that allowed the seats to fold back when they were not in use, the lighting arrangement that caused the butterfly curtains to change colour, the removable ashtrays. When we had perused all that, he gathered the plans and the sketches into a roll and secured them with a rubber band.

'The town will be the better,' Frau Messinger murmured, so softly that the remark was almost lost. People would delight in the cinema, she went on, her tone becoming a little louder. It would be a centre of life, as a church was. From miles around people would ride in on their bicycles for a few hours of relaxation; they would come in traps and jaunting-cars, and when the Emergency was over they would come in motor-cars.

'And, Harry, there is employment for you,' Herr Messinger interrupted. 'When you have finished at that school of yours.'

I looked astonished. He laughed.

'Why not, heh? Would you object to work for me? You choose instead to spend your lifetime with planks of wood? You have a brother, Harry?'

When I replied that I had two he nodded and went on doing so, one eye invisible behind the drooping lid. Since I had two brothers, he pointed out, there was a double reason why I should not be required in my father's business.

'I would place you in the box-office, Harry, to sell the tickets. Later on maybe to oversee the cleaning. To pay the wages of the usherettes. Soon you would learn, Harry. Soon we would learn together.'

My mother would consider that selling tickets in a cinema was inferior to taking my place in the timberyard. My mother's tongue became sharp in anger: having suffered pain and inconvenience bringing four children into the world she demanded sensibleness in return. My father would be bewildered and confused, as he was by any deviation from his own assumptions. 'Errah, get on with you, girl,' he'd said when Annie had wanted to go to Dublin to sell dresses in Arnott's or Switzer's. Wasn't she the luckiest girl in the town to have a decent position waiting for her in the accounts shed, with old Miss McLure ready to retire? My mother had been more forceful: she'd given Annie what she called 'a dressing down', pointing out that shop-work was on a par with being a skivvy, that the rest of the family would not be able to hold their heads above the disgrace of it. For days there'd been the sound of Annie's weeping and her blotched face at mealtimes. And, ever since, the sullenness had been part of her.

'So we are arranged,' Herr Messinger said, with confidence. 'Always, since we married, I have dreamed to make a gift like this. Imagine it, Harry, she married an old tortoise like me!' He laughed and kissed her. She clung to him for a moment, whispering something I could not hear. They laughed together; he lit another cigar. He said:

'She wants it to be nice for everyone. I want it to be nice for her. That is how a gift must be.' He went away with his roll of plans, and after a moment his wife offered me a cigarette. I leaned forward so that the flame of her circular cigarette-lighter might catch the tip of it. The brief touch of her fingers was as cold as marble. She said:

'I could not give him children.' Her smile continued to indulge him after he had left the room. Her own name was Alexandra, which was something I had not known before: even though she had failed him, he was offering her a gift which was to be created as she wished, to bring pleasure to strangers. All he asked was that, it seemed: the fulfilment of a whim in her.

'We can live without anything but love, Harry. Always remember that.'

Daphie brought in the tea, and it was poured. I was made to continue standing by the fire, although my clothes were dry by now and in any case would become damp again on my journey home. All the time, while she talked once more about her past, I thought about the offer that had been made to me. I could feel the cosy claustrophobia of the tiny office of the plans, the window in the glass, hands offering money. For the first time — I think the only time — I hardly listened to the childhood incidents related to me, to the speculations about her unknown father's appearance, the journeying through England and through Germany, and Bach mellifluous on the organ in that candlelit cathedral. There would be green tickets, and red and grey, and I would tear them off singly or in twos and threes; I would dole out pleasure to patrons of all ages.

Before I left that day she asked me to kiss her because it was Christmas Eve. I touched her cheek with my lips, and for a moment she slipped her hand into mine. Christmas would be quiet at Cloverhill, she said: she and her husband would exchange presents, and there were presents for Daphie and the workmen. They would sit together by the fire. 'And I have this for you, Harry.'

She gave me a tie-pin, a slender bar of gold. She'd found it years ago, she said, on one of her early-morning strolls about Münster. She'd seen it gleaming on a paving-stone, where someone had lost it the night before. 'I used to wonder about that person,' she said, 'but I haven't for a long time now. It's time I gave this away.'

She showed me how to pin it into my collar, beneath my tie, but on the way home I took it out in case it should again work itself loose. I have never worn it, fearing its loss, but often I take it from my dressing-table drawer and slip it for a moment into my collar before returning it to safety. Of all I have, it is my most treasured possession.

# THREE

*I*N THE NEW YEAR, workmen began the demolition of the two empty houses in the square and my brothers and I watched from a distance. Stones and bricks were carried away in lorries, the silver-painted railings that had rusted in front of the two gardens suddenly weren't there any more.

'Oh, the Hun boys don't let the grass grow,' my father said, knocking pepper over a plate of sausages in the dining-room. The timber for the new building was to be supplied from our yard, and for that he was naturally pleased, but he had not yet come to terms with Herr Messinger's decision to supply a town in which he was a stranger with a cinema. Between moments of attention paid to his sausages, he remarked upon the swift determination with which the German had acted. 'And isn't it a surprising thing, the way he'd have got the money out of Germany?'

'Did he send for it?' my mother enquired, without much interest.

'Errah, how could he, for God's sake? Isn't there a war raging over there?'

My mother never seemed offended by such scorn, appearing to accept it as her due, even nodding her agreement with it. But just occasionally, perhaps once or twice a year, her pusillanimity gave way to protest and in the privacy of their bedroom she could be heard spiritedly shouting abuse at my father, calling him uncouth and unclean, bitterly asserting she'd rather share a bed with an animal. His own voice in reply was always so mumbling and low that you couldn't hear properly what he said; but his tone suggested that he didn't deny her accusations, perhaps even promised to do better in the future.

'Is it she that has the money, boy? Did the woman ever tell you?'

I shook my head. I said I had obtained no knowledge of the Messingers' financial arrangements, or the source or distribution of their wealth. I was not telling the truth since I knew Frau Messinger to have been a poor relation, and her husband to be a member of a well-to-do family. None of that seemed anyone's business except their own; certainly it was not a tit-bit to be carried into the back bar of Viney's hotel.

'There's money there somewhere,' my father said.

We sat around the dining-room table, all of us eating sausages and fried bread, my grandmothers silently cantankerous with one another, my father airing his views. News he had heard during the day's business was imparted at this hour, anecdotes repeated, deaths and births announced.

'They were saying in Viney's,' he reported now, 'that there's marble on order for the front steps. Did you ever meet the beat of that, marble steps for a picture house!'

'Is it the Connemara marble?' my mother enquired.

'What else would it be? What's the price of Connemara, Annie?'

It was a delusion of my father's that because she kept the timberyard accounts Annie was conversant with the price of any commodity that had to do with the building trade.

'Corrugated, Annie?' he had a way of saying in the dining-room. 'What would I give for a three by six?' Further resentment in Annie would fester then, her face becoming even heavier in her resistance to all that was being foisted on her. 'Ah, sure, she's settled in well to the accounts,' I had heard him telling a man on the street one day. 'Sure, what more could she want?'

'When they have the picture house built,' one of my brothers asked, 'will they charge much to go in there?'

My mother told him not to speak with his mouth full of bread because no one could hear him properly. My father, to whom the same objection might have been put, said:

'I'd say they would. I'd say your man would need a big return on his money. What would he charge, Annie, to make sense of the thing?'

My sister said she had no idea. Briefly, she closed her eyes, endeavouring to dispose of my father and the ability she had ages ago been invested with as regards swift calculation. My father did not pursue the matter. Completing the consumption of another sausage, he turned to me.

'Did you ever find out are they Jews?'

'She's a Protestant. They were married in a Catholic cathedral.'

'I'd say you had it wrong.'

At that time of my life, harshly judging my father's opinions and statements, his dress, his clumsiness, his paucity of style, his manner of lighting a cigarette, I found it perhaps more difficult than I might have to forgive him for dismissing the answers I offered to his questions. In retrospect, of course, forgiveness is easier.

'That man's not rough enough to be a Catholic,' my mother put in.

[ 45 ]

The squatter of my two grandmothers asked us what we were talking about. In a raised voice my father replied that the man out at Cloverhill was going to build a new picture house for the town. 'I've nothing against a Jew-man,' he said. 'He has a head for business.'

'Isn't Colonel Hardwicke out at Cloverhill?' my grandmother asked. 'Running after the maids there?'

'Colonel Hardwicke's dead,' my father shouted, and my other grandmother nodded disdainfully. 'Dead as a doornail,' said my father.

My mother cut more bread. She poured tea into my father's cup. 'There's a picture they're after making in America that's four hours long,' he said. 'Did you hear about that one, Annie?'

'*Gone with the Wind.*'

'What's that, girl?'

'The name of the film is *Gone with the Wind.*'

'It was young Gerrity was telling me when he came into the yard. I'd say it was called something else.'

'*Gone with the Wind* is the only picture that's as long as that. It's coming to the Savoy in Dublin. There's people going up to see it.'

'Cripes!' one of my brothers exclaimed with enthusiasm. 'Wouldn't it be great to be in the pictures for four hours!'

Sharply, my mother told him not to say 'Cripes' in the dining-room. She reminded him that she'd given a warning in this respect before. My brothers were getting rougher with every day that went by, she said, glaring at both of them.

'Mr Wauchope'll knock it out of them.' My father confidently wagged his head, at the same time turning it in my direction. He winked at me. 'What's that big stick you were telling me about, that Mr Wauchope has in a cupboard?'

I looked at him dumbly, extreme denseness in my eyes. 'What stick's that?'

'Hasn't he a blackthorn for beating the living daylights out of any young fellow who'd misbehave himself?' He released a guffaw, winking at me a second time.

'He has a rod for closing the windows with. You can't reach the top part of the windows,' I explained to my brothers, 'so old Wauchope has to hook the end of a rod into them.'

'Is it Mr Conron I'm thinking of in that case?' my father persevered, his hand held up to disguise further winking from my brothers. One of my grandmothers asked him what the matter was, but he didn't answer her. 'Is it Mr Conron that lays into you with the blackthorn?'

'Conron wouldn't have the strength to hit anyone.' I paused, leisurely dividing a piece of fried bread into triangular segments. I imagined myself in the box-office, telling people who asked me that *Gone with the Wind* wouldn't end till one o'clock in the morning. 'Conron's a type of loony,' I told my brothers.

My father was taken aback. The grin that had been twitching about his lips gradually evaporated. Before I'd been sent to lodge in the rectory he used to read from a letter he'd received from the Reverend Wauchope which itemised the attractions of the boarding arrangements for Lisscoe grammar school. Around this same dining-table we had listened to elaborate inaccuracies about well-heated rooms and plentiful supplies of fresh vegetables from the rectory's own garden. The assistant master lodged at the rectory also, the letter said, so that discipline was maintained.

'That's the stupidest thing I ever heard in my life,' my father muttered crossly.

'A boy from Enniscorthy says Conron was in the loony place they have there. He used to roll a hoop along the road. He thought he was Galloping O'Hogan.'

'That's eejity talk, boy. Don't take any notice of it,' my father sternly advised my brothers.

'I'm only saying what I was told,' I said. 'You'd be sorry for poor Conron.'

'What's the trouble?' one of my grandmothers demanded, and I began to repeat all over again what I'd just told my brothers, but my father interrupted me and shouted at my grandmother not to waste her energy listening. 'No man could teach in a classroom if he was a lunatic. We've heard enough of it.' he said to me. 'Annie, did the pine come in?'

There was a film Houriskey had seen in which the main actor was employed in the box-office of a theatre when all the time he wanted to be on the stage. To make matters worse, he fell in love with an actress who passed by the box-office every night. That was the kind of thing you'd have to be careful about. You could become so familiar with a film actress on the screen that before you knew where you were you'd be in love with her, suffering like the actor, or poor Mandeville over the royal princess.

'What's this?' my mother demanded, two days after my slandering of the assistant master. She held in the palm of her hand Frau Messinger's Christmas present. I had hidden it under the drawer-paper in my bedroom.

'It's a tie-pin. You put it in your collar.'

'Where d'you get it?'

'I found it on the street.'

'That's a lie.'

'I found it outside Kickham's on Christmas Eve.'

'That isn't true.'

Tears pressed against my eyelids. I didn't know why they had come so suddenly, or why so urgently they demanded to be released. I realise now they were tears of anger.

'Why are you telling me lies?'

'They're not lies. Someone dropped the thing on the street.'

'Don't tell me lies on a Sunday, Harry. Did you steal it? Did you take it off someone at school?'

'I'm telling you I didn't.'

She stood there in her Sunday clothes, two patches of scarlet spreading on her cheeks, the way they always did when she was cross. I had entered the bedroom I'd once shared with Annie and now had for myself. She'd been there, with the drawer still open. What right had she to go looking in my drawers?

'Frau Messinger gave to me at Christmas.'

'*Mrs Messinger*?'

'Out at Cloverhill — '

'I know where the woman lives. Are you telling me the truth now?'

'Yes.'

'What'd she give you a Christmas present for?'

'She just gave it to me.'

'She gives you cigarettes too. You come back smelling of cigarettes.'

'I smoke the odd one.'

'If your father heard this he'd take the belt to you.'

I did not reply, and it was my mother who wept, not I. In her navy-blue, Sunday clothes she soundlessly wept and I watched the tears come from her eyes and run into the powder of the face she had prepared for going to church. Like Annie and like myself, she was tired of this house, of the two deaf old women who would not civilly address one another, of my father's lugubrious conversation, and my brothers' sniggering. I know that now, but at the time I had no pity for my mother's tears, and no compassion for her trapped existence. I wanted to hurt her because a secret I valued had been dirtied by her probing.

'You will give it back,' she commanded, her voice controlled, her tears wiped away with the tips of her fingers. 'You will give it back to the woman.'

'Why would I?'

'Because I'm telling you to. Because I'm ashamed of you, Harry, as you should be yourself.'

'I haven't done anything.'

'A woman that's not related to a young boy doesn't give him a present. I'm ashamed you would have taken it.'

'There's no harm in a tie-pin.'

My mother hit me. She slapped me across the face, the way she used to when I was younger than my brothers. A sting of pain lingered on the side of my cheek; my whole face tingled hotly.

'You'll give that back to her.'

I blinked, determined not to cry, looking away from her. The tie-pin was a present, I repeated. You couldn't give back a present.

'You'll give it back and you'll have done with going out to that house.' My mother went on talking, fast and angrily, calling Frau Messinger a wanton and a strumpet. 'Oh, a great time she has for herself, with young boys coming out to visit her. Amn't I the queer fool not to have known?'

I remained silent. I had no intention of returning the tie-pin, nor did I intend to discontinue my visits to Cloverhill. If my father knew about this, my mother said, he'd go out there himself and abuse the pair of them.

That wasn't true. My father would never have gone out to Cloverhill House in such a frame of mind, any more than he would have thrashed me with his belt. All during our childhood there had been this threat of my father's violence, but whenever some misdemeanour was reported to him he'd been bewildered and at a loss for words. He had taken no action whatsoever.

'Get ready for church,' my mother said.

Later, as we walked up through the town — my father and my brothers, Annie with my grandmothers — my mother said to me that none of them must know what had occurred, or hear anything whatsoever about the tie-pin. It would upset my brothers and sister, and worry my grandmothers; my father would be beside himself for a month. 'You'll be ashamed when you think about it in church,' she said.

I stared stonily ahead, at my father's back. On Sundays he wore a blue serge suit with a waistcoat, and a collar and tie, and an overcoat when it was cold. It was the only day of the week he looked like a Protestant, a respectable timberyard proprietor who had made his way up in the world, who carried coins in his pocket to distribute among us at the church gates. On other days he wore working clothes, since only they were suitable for the dust and grime of the yard. He still loaded timber himself, and worked the saws and planes. Occasionally he drove one of the lorries.

On the way to church he greeted people he knew among the Catholics coming back from late Mass, the women grasping their prayerbooks, men with collars and ties. You could tell at a glance they were different from us: they didn't often walk in a family as we did, but in ones and twos, with occasionally a huge bunch of children on their own, sprawled all over the street, chattering busily. The children eyed us, but because of my father and mother they didn't shout 'Proddy-woddy-green-guts' or 'dolled-up-heathens'. Our pace was slow because of the two old women, and we always had to leave the house early in order to allow for this. In the church it took them ages to sit down, fumbling and making certain they were as far away from one another as possible. Neither of them stood up for the psalm or the hymns, only for the Creed.

On that particular Sunday, while we progressed through the town and stood waiting in the aisle for my grandmothers to settle themselves, and later while my brothers fidgeted and poked at one another during the service, I continued to be aware of the impression of my mother's hand on the side of my face. I was not a child, I thought, to be struck so; I could not imagine Houriskey or Mahoney-Byron, or even Mandeville, undergoing such humiliation. And again I thought: what right had she to go searching under my drawer-paper?

I listened to my father mumbling the responses and wondered if she hit him in anger also; was a blow ever struck when they had their bedroom disagreements? I doubted it: her sharp tongue would do the work for her, it was children who were hit. Hundreds of times during my childhood I had planned to run away after receiving such punishment; here in this pew, not listening to the pulpit admonitions, I had seen myself arriving in a harbour town and slipping under a pile of canvas on a deck. They would be sorry then. I would be carried away, and white-faced and grief-stricken they would pray for my return.

'You'll go out with it this afternoon,' my mother said on

the walk home from church. 'And that'll be the end of the matter.'

She would find it no matter where I put it; not trusting me, she would search high and low. So I hid it at Cloverhill. I dropped it down a crevice between the hall-door steps, and then I pulled the bell-chain. I was shown into the drawing-room and soon afterwards tea was brought in by Daphie. I smoked three cigarettes.

That spring, at school, I received my first letter from Frau Messinger. Her handwriting was neat and sloping, slender loops on the letters that demanded them, dots and cross-strokes where they belonged. *It is such excitement, Harry! We drive in every day. I had not known that building anything could be so much fun.* Steel reinforcements were bathed in concrete, walls rose, rubble was levelled and floors laid down, rain fell on the workmen, the roof went on. *It has brought such joy to my husband, Harry, that so many people should come and stand by him and are pleased at what is happening. But, oh, how I long for it all to be finished, to sit and watch the screen!* 'Will the war be over first, or your picture house complete?' *a man said to my husband the other day. Once upon a time people were slow to mention the war to him, he being a German, but now all that has gone.*

I still have all her letters of that time, and when I read them now, as often I do, I believe I see Cloverhill as she had come to see it, and the town as she saw it also. In retrospect it is as easy to pass with her from room to room at Cloverhill as it is to keep company with the lanky child who visited the country houses of Sussex in the company of her diminutive mother, or the girl who met in Münster the old man she was to love. She told me once that all her life she had never slept well and as a child had always risen earlier than the servants in those well-servanted households, to explore places she did not have the courage to explore by day. Clearly, I see her. Her solitary figure wanders the morning streets of Münster. She is the first customer in a café; she reaches down a newspaper from its rack. I watch her unlocking the big hall-door of Cloverhill; I watch her descending the three steps on to the gravel sweep; the lawns on either side of it glistening with frost. *Harry will come today*: I have wondered, too, if that anticipation ever flickered in her mind as she strolled among the flower-beds, different in each season. *A boy from the town*: did she write that down in a letter to someone she once knew? Any boy would have done, or any girl: I don't delude myself. Yet so very poignantly I remember her kiss that Christmas Eve, and feel the coldness of the tie-pin passed into my hand. Once I gave her a present myself: two packets of American cigarettes. I bought them from a boy at the grammar school who used to sell such things, cigarettes having become excessively hard to obtain. 'Oh, Harry *darling*,' she said.

Often I am affected by memories of the Messingers together, memories that are theirs, not mine, as if the thrall they held me in has bequeathed such a legacy. Opposite one another at their teak dining-table, they seem quite dramatically an old man and a girl, he entertaining her with an account of the work there has been on the farm that day, her turn now to listen. In their bedroom, they undress and fold their clothes away, the summer twilight not yet night. In their breakfast-room he opens letters while they drink black coffee. Logs blaze and crackle; the sun warms the conservatory that opens off the room. There is music on their wireless.

Later, wrapped up against the weather, they move through the void of the building they have talked about, their footsteps echoing. For the interior walls they choose the shades of amber that later became familiar to me, darker at the bottom, lightening to dusty paleness as the colour spreads over the ceiling. These walls must be roughly textured, they decree, the concave ceiling less so, the difference subtly introduced. Four sets of glass swing-doors catch a reflection of the marble steps that so astonished my father: the doors between the foyer and the auditorium are of the warm mahogany supplied by our timberyard. Long before the building is ready for it, they choose the blue-patterned carpet of the balcony, and the scarlet cinema-seats.

Herr Messinger drives the gas-powered car back to Cloverhill; she leans a little tiredly on his arm as together they enter the house. In the town they have bought things for their lunch. 'We often have just a tin of sardines. Meals should be picnics, don't you think, Harry?'

Time passed. At school the same jokes continued. In the Reverend Wauchope's rectory fat Lottie Belle waddled the same plates of unpleasant food from the kitchen to the discoloured oilcloth spread over the dining-table. At home my father's conversation was changelessly pursued. 'We like this friendship we have made,' Frau Messinger said in her drawing-room.

One April day, when I returned from Lisscoe more than a year after work had first begun on the cinema, I sensed that something was wrong. The building appeared to have reached a standstill. I did not question my father or Annie about this, as I might have done, but instead, continuing to ignore my mother's strictures, walked out to Cloverhill. 'She's sick,' Daphie said, opening the white hall-door to me. 'She's taken to her bed.'

There was no sign of Herr Messinger in the fields or on the avenue and when I returned a week later, to be met by the same response, he was not in evidence either. Nor, to my surprise, did he once appear in the square, though he had regularly done so in the past. Frau Messinger's last letter had not mentioned illness, but had referred as usual to their visiting the building works together. In my frustration I became depressed, was chided by my father for being down-in-the-mouth and made to shovel sawdust in the timberyard, which he said would cheer me up. Then, on the day before I was to return to school, I heard Herr Messinger's voice as I passed his half-completed building. 'But *always* I wait,' he was protesting disconsolately. 'Always I say make haste and always you promise. You are letting me down when I cannot come in every day.'

The builder, a companion of my father's in the back bar of Viney's, began his reassurances. He was doing his best in every hour God sent him; the only trouble was there was an emergency in the country. Materials could not be obtained in the usual manner or at the usual speed. If he'd been asked to construct a cinema five years ago the entire population of the neighbourhood would have been watching Mickey Mouse within a six-month.

'This is moving from the point, though. Since I haven't been able to visit the site your men have slowed down, heh?'

'There's no better men in the land, sir.'

'If they could just be a little swifter on their feet, maybe?'

Turning away for a moment, perhaps to hide his exasperation, Herr Messinger saw me standing there. He nodded, but didn't smile or address me. I'd never known him so uncommunicative.

'I'll tell you what, sir.' Thoughtfully the builder passed a hand over the stubble of his jaw. 'Come back on Thursday and you won't know the place.'

He was a bigger man than Mr Messinger and having completed the massage of his jaw he placed the same hand on the German's shoulder, bending a little to do so. A smile of satisfaction rippled the ham-like complacency of his features. 'I had to pacify the old Hun,' I imagined him saying to my father in the back bar. 'Sure, haven't the poor men only the one pair of legs to each of them?' My father would be duly sympathetic: in the dining-room he had often related how he had similarly extricated himself from the complaints of a customer about a delay due to some oversight in the timberyard.

Herr Messinger said he would return before Thursday; he would return tomorrow; not a day would pass from now on without a visit from him at the building site. In a way that reminded me of my father also, the builder said he'd be welcome. Wasn't it the man who pays the piper that calls the tune? he amiably remarked. When he'd ambled off Herr Messinger spoke to me.

'Well, Harry, so you are back again?'

'Yes.'

'Harry, she is not well. The early months she hates before spring comes. Well, that is wrong, so she says: it is the early months that don't like her. January, February, March too. And this year she was determined to watch the building. So the months took their revenge, Harry.'

'Is she getting better?'

'When you return for the summer you will see for yourself.' He smiled at me; gold glistened in his teeth. 'Oh,

Harry, these labourers do not advance much. And then of course it is true: commodities are hard to come by in the Emergency. The architect does not arrive because he has no petrol, and I myself — well, I like to be with her when she is not all right.'

'Please thank her for her letters.'

'When you go back to your school she will write a few more. As she improves, so summer comes again.'

'I'd write back only it's hard to get stamps where I am.'

'Don't worry about writing back.'

'She never said she was ill.'

'That wouldn't be her way, Harry.'

He strode away, dapper in his German clothes, the shine of his gaiters catching the sunlight. Later that morning, in Nagle Street, he waved to me from his car. I wished he'd said that I might visit her in her bedroom. I had thought he might say that: it would be ages now before I saw her.

For her sake I welcomed the mild weather of spring that year, and the warmth of early summer. During the dragging weeks of June there was a heatwave. Was it in June that anemones came? I had no idea.

'You will remember for ever your days in the rectory,' the Reverend Wauchope finally predicted, which were the words of his parting to all the pupils who boarded there. He was, of course, right. 'We will pray to God,' he said, and together he and I did so, he speaking for me, requesting guidance and the blessing of humility in the days of my future. 'I am to understand that you have failed to find affinity with scholarship,' he remarked. 'Nor have you otherwise achieved distinction. Your father is a draper, is he?'

'He has a timberyard, sir.'

'And a place for yourself in it? You are most fortunate. More fortunate than most.'

I did not reply. *After we have died*, the first letter I received during that term had asked, *do you believe there will be a heaven?* Subsequent letters referred to the possibility of this future also; the past, always previously her subject, was not touched upon. Nor was the present: for all the mention there was of it, the building of the cinema might have been defeated by the builder's lassitude and the shortages of the Emergency. The more I searched the lines of the letters for any hint of progress the more I experienced bleak dismay. Instead, repeated often, Frau Messinger had written: *I have never understood how it is we shall be separated, some of us for heaven, some for hell.*

'I have asked you a question,' the Reverend Wauchope said.

'I'm sorry, sir.'

'Do you intend to honour me with an answer?'

'I did not hear the question, sir.'

Only three letters had come; all had to do with life after death. A week ago the last one had arrived, urging a visit from me as soon as I returned. *The sweet-pea will be in flower and we might walk in the garden.*

'You appear to be inane,' the Reverend Wauchope said. His dry, scratchy voice querulously dismissed me without my having said — as I think I had intended to — that the timberyard did not attract me. But the silence surrounding the Alexandra cinema made me apprehensive about continuing to consider it an alternative. Already I had convinced myself that it had been abandoned because of the illness that was not mentioned. Herr Messinger had lost heart in his gift.

'You are suitable for work with timber,' was the clergyman's final insult, the last thing he ever said to me.

With my three companions of the rectory I walked around the field where the cows grazed, Mandeville confessing that he'd been offered a position in a seed firm, Houriskey and Mahoney-Byron that they'd be going on to their fathers' farms. 'Oh yes, the timberyard,' I said. Mandeville wondered if we'd ever meet again: we thought we probably wouldn't.

Later, in an empty classroom of the school, I gathered together the dog-eared textbooks that had also been my companions for so long and returned them to Mr Conron. Staring hard at some point of interest on the floor, he warned me to be careful in Dublin if one day I should visit it. 'Take care with the women of the quays. Don't be tempted by quayside women.' With these words he offered an explanation for the torment that haunted his features. He lived with shame, yet some part of him was obliged surreptitiously to display its source, half proud confession, half punishment of himself. 'I'll take care all right,' I promised.

I tipped Lottie Belle the two shillings the Reverend Wauchope laid down as a suitable sum for all his boarders to pass on to her, the accumulation of such amounts reputed to constitute the major part of her wages. Mrs Wauchope, who had not addressed me during my years in the rectory, did not do so now.

On a morning in the middle of that same June heatwave I left Lisscoe for ever. The bus halted to drop off bundles of newspapers or to pick up the passengers who stood waiting at a crossroads or outside wayside public houses, or nowhere in particular. Towns passed through were similar to my own or just a little larger. Cattle drowsed in the fields, familiar landmarks slipped by. The bus was dusty and hot, its air pungent with the fumes of petrol; once it stopped because a woman was feeling sick. I wondered if I would ever make a journey anywhere again, if I was seeing for the last time the ruins by the river, the bungalow embedded with seaside shells, the green advertisement for Raleigh bicycles on the gable-end of a house: my father boasted that he was none the worse for having never in his life been on a bus. *We live and then we are forgotten*, she had written. *Surely that cannot be the end of us?* In the bus I re-read the three letters I had most recently received, phrases and paragraphs already known to me by heart. *A gravestone gathers lichen, flowers rot in the grave-vase.* In her drawing-room I could not recall her having once even touched upon this subject. She had not, for instance, speculated on the after-life of her dead mother, even though it was apparent from all she said that she had been more than ordinarily fond of her. She had not, when deploring the deaths of so many young soldiers in the war, ever wondered if that was truly the end of them.

The bus drew up by the martyr's statue in the square, taking me unawares because the melancholy nature of my thoughts still absorbed me. The bus conductor handed down my single, heavy suitcase from the luggage rack on the roof, and then I was aware of the reddish tinge of a building that made the square seem different. In bright sunlight I gazed at a façade that was exactly as it had been on the architect's sketch, the baskets of flowers hanging from a hugely jutting ledge that formed a roof above the marble steps. *The Alexandra* proclaimed stylish blue letters, as if her hand had written them across the concrete.

# FOUR

*T*HE FLUSH IN HER CHEEKS was like the pink that may creep into the petals of a rose that should be purely white. She lay on her sofa, exactly as she had in the past, smoking and dispensing tea. It was a Sunday afternoon.

'I think you understand everything now, Harry?'

I shook my head but today she did not, as in the past, ignore my responses in our conversation. She observed my gesture, and smiled a little. She said:

'Everything here, Harry? All there has been at Cloverhill?'

'No,' I said.

'The cinema will open in a fortnight. With *Rebecca*. Harry, do you know *Rebecca*?'

She spoke lightly and with her usual casualness, but already I knew that death was everywhere in the drawing-room, and when I walked with her in the garden it was present also. The sweet-pea blooms were a trellis of colour — a dozen shades of purple and mauve, reds lightening and deepening, pinks and whites. Yellow hung from the laburnum shrubs, scarlet dotted the rose bushes. Yet the beauty of the Englishwoman chilled the blaze. Like a ghost sensed coldly, the melancholy of time deserting her was everywhere in the garden, as it had been in the drawing-room.

'Sweet-pea is my second favourite,' she said, and I could

tell she knew that at last my density had been penetrated. 'Sweet-pea in a cut-glass vase, set off by the fern of asparagus.'

We walked slowly among the flower-beds. Occasionally she bent down to pull out a weed. Mignonette was her third favourite, she said, but only because of its fragrance.

'I knew nothing about a garden when first we came to Cloverhill,' she said. 'He rescued it for me, you know.'

Brambles had flourished among the rhododendrons and the blue hydrangeas then, cornus was rampant. Fuchsia roots and bamboos had spread beneath the earth, escallonia was smothered. Her husband had dug the flower-beds out; he had discovered lost japonica, he had teased the straggles of jasmine back to health.

'I helped of course, Harry, but sometimes the work was heavy. And there was the farm as well.'

All that had been happening at the time of my first visits to Cloverhill. 'Look at that,' Herr Messinger had said once, showing me his hands, begrimed and scratched, nails broken, the pigment of vegetation colouring his palms. And often from the drawing-room window I had seen him dragging from the garden a cart loaded high with the undergrowth he had cut out. I had hardly noticed, I had not been interested; I had passed through the bedraggled garden without respecting its slow recovery.

'It would be nice to have that time again, Harry, I often think. To go back to the first day we arrived at Cloverhill, waiting in the emptiness for our furniture. We walked about the garden and through the fields. "There is a world to do," he said, and in my happiness I embraced him because I knew he loved to do things. It would be nice to experience again the afternoon you first came here, when Daphie said to me,

"There is a visitor." How shy you were, Harry! You hardly said a thing.'

Our progress had slowed down. She took my arm to lean on. We crossed the gravel sweep and went around the side of the house, finally reaching the lawn on to which the drawing-room French windows opened.

'That may be what heaven is, Harry: dreaming through times that have been. Tea in the drawing-room, and how you listened to my silly life!'

We stepped through the French windows, but she did not move towards the sofa. Instead she held her cheek out for me to kiss, and said when I had done so:

'If heaven is there, Harry.'

I was alone then in the room, and some intuition insisted that I had been with her for the last time, and for the last time had heard her voice. And yet as soon as these thoughts occurred I denied them, for how on earth could I know anything of the kind?

As I made my way down the avenue, Herr Messinger called to me from a field, where he was forking hay with one of his men. I clambered over the white-painted iron railing and crossed to where they worked. He came to meet me as I approached.

'Are you finished now at school, Harry?'

'Yes, I am finished now.'

'Well, that is good. You will work for me when the cinema is ready, heh? A fortnight, Harry.'

'Yes, I will work for you.'

'It has taken so long. How often I lost heart!'

I tried to say I was glad he hadn't, because I knew that without his energy and his determination the cinema would still be only half-built. I stumbled in my speech, finding the sentiments difficult to express.

'Ah, well, Harry.' He shook his head and turned away. She had been given a cinema because in such circumstances the giving of a gift had to be as great. And naturally he had wanted it to be swiftly completed. 'Herr Messinger,' I called after him, which was something I would have been too shy to do in the past. 'Herr Messinger, would you like me to assist you with the hay?'

He nodded very slightly, not turning to face me, and so I remained, working in silence beside him and his employee. When twilight came, and darkened, we did not cease because there was mown hay still lying. At home they would wonder where I was, and would be angry. All unusual behaviour made them angry. But as the moon rose and we piled up the last of the haycocks I didn't care about any of that.

'Come back to the house, Harry,' Herr Messinger said when he had finished. 'You are surely hungry.'

So I accompanied him on the avenue and around to the back of the house, across a yard I had never seen before, and into the kitchen. He lit a lamp because there was no electricity at Cloverhill. He placed it in the centre of the scrubbed wooden table.

'She'll have gone to bed,' he said. 'We're on our own, Harry.'

His workman had ridden off on a bicycle, and I thought it honourable the way Herr Messinger had thanked him so genuinely for working on a Sunday and had said there would be something extra in his wages. In the kitchen he said it was Daphie's evening off. There was a potato salad already prepared, he said, and cold meats with lettuce and tomatoes.

He hoped that would be sufficient for us. And wine, he remembered, not very good wine, but he had a little in the larder. 'The chromium for the foyer is to arrive tomorrow,' Herr Messinger said. 'And all the seating at the end of the week.'

We ate cold chicken and pork, and the salad. The wine was the colour of very pale straw, the first wine I had ever tasted; I thought it delicious. 'Ever since I knew her, Harry,' Herr Messinger suddenly said.

His square, hard face was solemn, though there were still crinkles of what I'd always taken to be amusement around his eyes. She would be asleep already, he said; she could not manage food in the evenings. He took tiny amounts on his fork, lifting the fork slowly to his mouth and then replacing it for a moment on his plate, sipping his wine.

'An old man marries for the time that is left, Harry. Both of us seemed not to have much time. Well, there you are.'

I was not hungry; I did not any longer want the pale-straw wine. But he, of course, was used to things being as they were, and ate and drank as usual. I had no knowledge of death; I had never experienced its sorrow or its untimely shock. 'Well, that was sudden,' my father would say before sitting down in the dining-room, and then reveal the name of a person who had died. 'God's mercy,' the Reverend Wauchope's scratchy voice would plead in the prayers to do with losses in the war. Shops closed their doors when a funeral crept by, the blinds of windows drawn down to honour the flower-laden coffin, the hooves of black-plumed horses the only sound.

Herr Messinger lit one of his small cigars. In silence he made coffee. I lifted from the table the plates off which we had eaten and placed them on the draining-board by the sink. I ran the tap but he said that Daphie would attend to all that when she returned. He spoke again of his wife.

'She will see the cinema open its doors. I know that in my heart and she in hers. She will taste the promise of its nights of pleasure. It worried her that we would only come and go at Cloverhill.'

He handed me my coffee, and pushed the sugar nearer. I saw the tears on her cheeks in the moment when she realised she must not marry the young man who had taken her to the poppy field. Had that broken her heart? I wondered.

'You must not worry yourself, Harry.'

'I'm only sorry.'

'The last months would have been empty if there had not been the building. Emptiness is the enemy.'

Soon after that I left. The night was warm, the moon a clear disc, untroubled by clouds. I had never before seen Cloverhill at night, and when I stopped to look back at the house I did not want to turn my gaze away. A pale sheen lightened the familiar grey façade and, in a way that seemed almost artificial, related trees and stone. Blankly, the dark windows returned my stare, a sightless pattern, elegant in the gloom. Did she suffer pain? I wondered.

'Where d'you get to, boy?' my father enquired, calling out to me from the dining-room. 'What time of the night is this to be coming in?'

I stood in the doorway. I could hear my mother rattling dishes in the kitchen, and a moment later she entered the dining-room with a tray of cups and saucers for the breakfast. My father was slouched in one of the old rexine-covered chairs by the fire-place, his slippered feet resting on the grate. Newspaper and kindling would remain unlit in the grate until

October, when this positioning of my father's feet would not be possible. Sometimes he forgot and scorched his slippers.

'Your mother's beside herself, boy. Were you drinking or what?'

'Frau Messinger's dying,' I said, but neither of them responded. My food had been ready at half-past six, my mother said; every day, Sundays included, that was the time. She wasn't a maid in her own house, she said; she wasn't a servant. 'Half-six,' my father repeated. 'If you want your grub half-six is the hour, boy.'

My mother took the saucers singly from the pile on her tray, and placed on each an inverted cup. She took cork mats from a drawer in the sideboard and laid the table with knives and forks and side plates. She didn't say anything, but listened while my father repeated what had been established already. He informed me that a meal had been fried for me and had sat in the oven until it was burnt. A waste of food that had already been paid for, he said, and hadn't my mother more to do than pander to the comings and goings of a youth? He reminded me it was a Sunday, the day of the week when my mother might be given an easy time. With painful deliberation he pressed open a packet of ten Sweet Afton and withdrew a cigarette, appearing to select one. 'Where were you drinking?' he said.

'I wasn't drinking.'

'You have drink taken, boy. You brought a smell of it into the house.'

'I had a glass of wine.'

My father scraped a match along the sandpaper of a matchbox. He examined the flame before raising it to his cigarette.

'Wine?'

'Yes.'

'You were out with those people,' my mother said.

'Where're you going now for yourself?' my father demanded, noticing that I had made a move.

'Up to bed.'

'Will you listen to that! As cool as water and the whole house after being in a turmoil!'

'You gave me a promise you wouldn't go out there.' My mother had suddenly become still. With a fork in her hand, her eyes hotly probed mine.

'I didn't promise anything,' I said.

I could see her deciding to cross the room to hit me, then deciding against it. My father said I'd had a good education, that money he couldn't spare had been spent on me. 'That food was taken out of the oven at twenty past eight,' he said. 'There isn't a dog in the town would have thanked you for it.'

'You promised me that day.' My mother did not take her eyes off me; I thought she hated me because I could feel something like hatred coming across the room from her.

'I nearly went down to the Guards,' my father said. My grandmothers couldn't touch their fried eggs, so that was more food wasted. It was the worst evening of my grandmothers' lives.

'There was an understanding between us.' She would stand there for ever, I thought, looking at me like that, as still as stone while my father tediously gabbled.

'Keep off the drink, boy,' he commanded, having issued other orders, as well as warnings and advice. 'You're too young for that game.'

'I'm going to work in the picture house.'

The vituperation I had anticipated burst simultaneously out of them, scornful and immediate. Their faces reddened. My father pushed himself on to his feet.

'I don't like it in the timberyard,' I said.

'What don't you like, boy?'

'I don't like any of it.'

'You're a young pup. Haven't you caused enough damage for one day? Go up and knock on your grandmothers' doors and tell them you're safe and sound. The other stuff you're talking about is rubbish.'

I went away, glad to be allowed to do so. Obediently I knocked on my grandmothers' doors, but there was no response from either of them, as I had known there wouldn't be. In my own room I sat on the edge of my bed and within a few moments I felt tears on my cheeks. In the dining-room they would be deploring my defiance, saying they could not control me, that I had always been like that, a bad example to my brothers. There had been pain in my father's eyes, and in the bluster of his voice when he'd called me a young pup, but I didn't care; I didn't care in the least how much I hurt them. It was like a nightmare, that she was going to die.

## FIVE

$S$LOWLY, CAREFULLY, she passed upstairs to the balcony, holding on to her husband's arm. And when *Rebecca* came to an end they left the cinema in the same unhurried manner. There was, I realise now, nothing she might have said to me, and I could tell from her expression that she found it difficult to smile. 'Please wait,' Herr Messinger had requested when he'd set out my duties for that evening. He returned some time later, and together we locked up his property. 'One day I shall place you in charge of the Alexandra,' he said. He paused, and added: 'That is her wish, and my own too.'

I would have carried the wireless battery out to Cloverhill as I had before, but that was not suggested. At a quarter past ten every night Herr Messinger arrived in his gas-powered motor-car and stood on the marble steps, ready to say goodnight to his customers when the film ended. I believe, although I cannot be certain, that she asked him to. When everyone had gone I would give him the cash-box and he would drive away again.

Three times a week I fetched the films in their metal cases from the railway station and returned those that had been shown, the smaller cases containing the newsreels and the shorts, another episode of *Flaming Frontiers* or *The Torture Chamber of Doctor R.* Every evening, and during the Sunday matinee, I sat in the projection room with the old man who had been the projectionist in some other town, whom Herr Messinger had brought back into employment. When the old man's stomach gave him trouble and he wasn't able to come in I took his place, as soon as there was no further custom at the box-office.

'For the sake of your mother,' my father pleaded, 'wouldn't you have a bit of sense for yourself?'

He meant wouldn't I stop doing what I was content to do and return to the drabness of the timberyard. I was becoming a queer type of a fellow, he told me, which wasn't a good thing for a mother to have to see. 'Come into Viney's one day and we'll have a bottle of stout over it,' he invited, forgetting his advice to me with regard to drinking in public houses.

Politely, I thanked him and said I'd look into Viney's when I had a moment to spare, not intending to and in fact never doing so. On the balcony stairs there were framed photographs of William Powell and Myrna Loy, of Loretta Young and Carole Lombard and Norma Shearer, of Franchot Tone and Lew Ayres. I could see some of them from the box-office and used to watch people stopping to examine them, couples arm in arm, the girls' voices full of wonder. In the mornings I opened the exit doors at the back, on either side of the screen, in order to let the fresh air in for an hour or two. When the woman who swept the place out didn't arrive I did it myself; I mopped the foyer and the steps, and went over the carpets with the suction cleaner. Often in the mornings I would press the switch that caused the yellow and green curtains that obscured the screen to open, the butterflies of the pattern disappearing as the curtains moved. When the daylight came in through the exit doors the amber shading of the walls seemed different.

People loved the Alexandra. They loved the things I loved myself — the scarlet seats, the lights that made the curtains change colour, the usherettes in uniform. People stood smoking in the foyer when they'd bought their tickets, not in a hurry because smoking and talking gave them pleasure also. They loved the luxury of the Alexandra, they loved the place it was. Urney bars tasted better in its rosy gloom; embraces were romantic there. Fred Astaire and Ginger Rogers shared their sophisticated dreams, Deanna Durbin sang. Heroes fell from horses, the sagas of great families yielded the riches of their secrets. Night after night in the Alexandra I stood at the back, aware of the pleasure I dealt in, feeling it all around me. Shoulders slumped, heads touched, eyes were lost in concentration. My brothers did not snigger in the Alexandra; my father, had he ever gone there, would have at last been silenced. Often I imagined the tetchiness of the Reverend Wauchope softening beneath a weight of wonder, and the sour disposition of his wife lifted from her as she watched *All This and Heaven Too*. Often I imagined the complicated shame fading from the features of Mr Conron. 'I have told her you are happy,' Herr Messinger said.

Annie began to come to the cinema with young Phelan from Phelan's grocery, in whose presence she was less sullen. She showed him off, one eye on me in the box-office, pausing on the balcony stairs and calling out loudly to people she knew. She had begun to wear different shades of lipstick, and had her hair done in a different way. For all my good fortune in being sent away to school, and my escape from the timberyard, she would outdo me in the end. She was outdoing me already, her manner implied, standing close to young Phelan.

A month before the war ended the death took place at

Cloverhill House. Herr Messinger did not mention it but I knew it had occurred because he arrived at the cinema in mourning, and two days later there was the funeral, her body taken to our Protestant graveyard. He made arrangements about the sale of his land and the running of the cinema, placing certain matters in the hands of McDonagh and Effingham, the solicitors, others in the care of the Münster and Leinster Bank. It was not clear then that one day I would become the cinema's proprietor, that arrangements had been made in this respect also. 'I'd say you landed on your feet,' my father grudgingly remarked when the big attendances the cinema had begun to attract showed no sign of abating, but my mother never forgave me for rejecting my heritage in favour of selling tickets, and for ignoring her wishes. When my mother lay dying in 1961 she referred again to Frau Messinger as a wanton and a strumpet, whose grave she knew I tended, growing anemones on the humped earth.

My mother was right when she sensed the need to be jealous. Frau Messinger had claimed me from the moment she stepped from her husband's car that day in Laffan Street; and she had held me to her with the story of her life. Details that were lost in the enchantment of her voice return with time. How when she was five she picked a flower from a garden where she was a visitor, and afterwards felt a thief. How she overheard servants being cruel about her mother. How she had bathed in a shrubbery lake, before anyone else was up, the water so petrifyingly cold she'd thought she could not bear it. How the old man said to her the first time she met him, in a German bookshop furnished like a drawing-room: 'Have you read *Wanderers Nachtlied*?' She hadn't even heard of it, and blushed with shame.

I retrieved her present from the crevice in the step at

Cloverhill. All the windows already had boards on them, efficiently nailed into place, as though Herr Messinger wished to keep the contents of the house exactly as they were, unaffected even by sunlight. The land was sold and farmed by someone else; Daphie went to work for other people. I was given the task – for which I was remunerated once a month through the solicitors – of seeing that the window boards remained in place and were renewed when necessary, and that the doors were kept secure. It was everyone's belief – the solicitors', the bank's, his employees' at the cinema – that Herr Messinger intended to return, that once again he would root out the brambles from the garden and let light into the drawing-room. I knew he never would. He could not be alone in Cloverhill. In Germany he would be hopelessly searching for his sons.

## SIX

MY BROTHERS run the timberyard, my sister married Phelan, my father went the way of my mother and my grandmothers. I do not forget those family mealtimes, the half bottle of whiskey kept in the sideboard in case anyone had toothache, holly poked behind the pictures at Christmas. I do not forget my companions of the rectory bedroom, nor poor obese Lottie Belle, who did not then seem worthy of compassion. I do not forget them, but even so I do not dwell much on those particular memories. Is such love reserved for the dying? I ask myself instead, and do not know the answer.

Years ago the butterfly curtains had to be taken down because they were rotting. When you listen with your ear to the boarded windows of Cloverhill you can hear the rats inside. One day next week men will place corrugated iron over the entrance to the cinema, and over the exit doors at the back. I shall not sell the place, even though I have been tempted with a fair price from a business partnership that would turn it into a furniture store; in the town I am considered foolhardy because I have rejected this offer. I am considered odd, being so often seen on the Ballinadee road on my way to tap the window boards, making certain they are sound. In the town it is said that the cinema has destroyed me, that I'd have been better off if I'd never inherited it in that peculiar way. My sister and brothers have said it to my face, others have whispered. I am pitied because I am solitary and withdrawn, because I have not taken my place and am left in the end with nothing. I have no answer.

It is sad that through a quirk of fashion no one came much to the Alexandra these last few years. It is sad that rats are in charge at Cloverhill. But a husband's love and a woman's gratitude for sanctuary have not surrendered their potency. I am a fifty-eight-year-old cinema proprietor without a cinema, yet when I sit among the empty seats memory is enough. She smiles from the green-striped cushions, he spreads his drawings on the floor. My rain-soaked clothes drip on to the fender by the fire, there is happiness in spite of death and war. Fate has made me the ghost of an interlude: once in a while I say that in the town, trying to explain.